Still Life

THE CHESHIRE PRIZE FOR LITERATURE ANTHOLOGIES

Prize Flights: Stories from the Cheshire Prize for Literature 2003; edited by Ashley Chantler

Life Lines: Poems from the Cheshire Prize for Literature 2004; edited by Ashley Chantler

Word Weaving: Stories and Poems for Children from the Cheshire Prize for Literature 2005; edited by Jaki Brien

Edge Words: Stories from the Cheshire Prize for Literature 2006; edited by Peter Blair

Elements: Poems from the Cheshire Prize for Literature 2007; edited by Peter Blair

Wordscapes: Stories and Poems for Children from the Cheshire Prize for Literature 2008; edited by Jaki Brien

Zoo: Short Stories from the Cheshire Prize for Literature 2009; edited by Emma Rees

Still Life

Poems from the Cheshire Prize for Literature 2010

Edited by Emma Rees

University of Chester Press

First Published 2011
by University of Chester Press
Parkgate Road
Chester CH1 4BJ

Printed and bound in the UK by the
LIS Print Unit
University of Chester
Cover designed by the LIS Graphics Team
University of Chester

Foreword and Editorial Material
© University of Chester, 2011
Poems
© the respective authors, 2011
Front cover image
Luiz Meléndez, Still Life with Oranges and Walnuts
© The National Gallery, London

All Rights Reserved
No part of this publication may be reproduced, stored in a retrieval system or transmitted in any form or by any means without the prior permission of the copyright owner, other than as permitted by UK copyright legislation or under the terms and conditions of a recognised copyright licensing scheme

A catalogue record of this book is available
from the British Library

ISBN 978-1-905929-88-7

For Saf

CONTENTS

Contributors	xiii
Foreword	xxx
Still Life with Oranges and Walnuts (Luis Meléndez) *Rita Ray*	1
Diptych *Philip Williams*	3
The Cupboard Under the Stairs *Jennifer Anne Durban*	4
Hide and Seek *Heather Freckleton*	6
Haiku Moments *Sheila Powell*	8
Furniture Complex *Anna Mackenzie*	9
Worms *George Horsman*	10
Spellbound *Clive McWilliam*	11

Ada in the Garden *Clive McWilliam*	12
Burning the Clothes *Frances Sackett*	13
Shoreline *Frances Sackett*	14
Twelve Men and a Cheeseboard *Linda Houlton*	15
Threads *James Phillips*	17
The Careers Master *Simon Gotts*	20
Grasshopper Girl *Jean Page*	22
Cotton Atlas *Jean Page*	23
Paper Patterns *Angela Topping*	24
Moon Walk *Frances Sackett*	25
Amaryllis *Philip Watts*	26

Early Sparrow-Grass *Liz Loxley*	27
Pontoon *Liz Loxley*	28
Sloe Gin *Liz Loxley*	29
Darwin's Finches *Rob Blaney*	30
The Migrant *Angi Holden*	31
Rook and Jackdaw Migrations Observed in Germany 1942–1945 *Richard Hughes*	32
The Lure *Caroline Hawkridge*	34
Wings, Planes and Weather Vanes *Joy Winkler*	36
Grandparents *Ruth Symes*	37
The History Department *Anne-Marie Biggs*	38
An Orphan at Thirty Six *Barbara Holliday*	40

Icon *Peter Branson*	41
Jazz on Nine Eleven *Rob Blaney*	42
Massage *George Horsman*	44
Temple Garden *Jonathan Musgrove*	45
Crossing: 1946 *Russell Morris*	46
Crosby Sands – An Iron Man Speaks *Ellis Lloyd*	47
Helsby in Winter Sun *Ellis Lloyd*	49
At Jodrell Bank *David Selzer*	51
Warrington Bank Quay *Catherine Bruton*	52
Quarry *Philip Williams*	55
Duke's Clough *Angela Topping*	56

Fog *Peter Howard*	57
Salt *Andrew Bailey*	58
A Fourth Dimension *Alison Leonard*	59
Sheep *Sheila Powell*	61
Recall *Angi Holden*	62
Horeb *Robbie Burton*	63
Dodo *Jonny Reid*	64
Mending Your Guitar *John Davies*	67
Yeats Exhibition *John Davies*	68
My Granddad Buries King at Souter Lighthouse *Jake Campbell*	69
Lunet (Friction Drum) *Judy Ugonna*	71

Slit Drum   72
Judy Ugonna

Jake   73
Jonny Reid

Teenagers in Love   74
Vikki Littlemore

Snagging   75
Michael Scully

Gerris lacustris (Common Pond Skater)   76
Helen Clare

Anax imperator (Emperor Dragonfly)   77
Helen Clare

THE CONTRIBUTORS

Andrew Bailey grew up near Northwich, with a first poetry publication credit in the school newsletter of Hartford County Primary School. He has since lived and worked over several counties, including time with the Poetry Society, the Poetry Archive and a couple of touring theatre companies. Poems have appeared in *Stand*, *Brittle Star*, *The Rialto*, *Poetry Review* and various online publications. He is a winner of *Poetry Review*'s Geoffrey Dearmer Prize.

Anne-Marie Biggs spent much of her life in Cheshire. She lived in Lymm and Bowdon as a child then, after some years away, moved back to Stockport and more recently to Macclesfield. She has now relocated to Warwickshire and misses the wide Cheshire skies (but not the rain). She enjoys writing fiction and would like to devote more time to it, although having two small children and working as a research manager make this challenging. She is currently working on an invention to expand the number of hours available in a day.

Rob Blaney was born and brought up in Alsager, south Cheshire. He works for a housing association, and has worked previously for homeless charities. His poetry has been published in an assortment of poetry magazines. In 2010 he gained an MA in Creative Writing from the University of Chester which motivated him to complete his first novel, *Soldier Bee* (as yet unpublished), and he is now working on a second, a political satire called *The Party*.

Peter Branson, a former teacher and lecturer, now organises writers' workshops in the North Staffordshire/South Cheshire region. His poetry has been published by journals in Britain, USA, Canada, Eire, Australia and New Zealand, including *Acumen*, *Ambit*, *Envoi*, *The London Magazine*, *Iota*, *Frogmore Papers*, *The Interpreter's House*, *Poetry Nottingham*, *South*, *The New Writer*, *Crannog*, *The Raintown Review*, *Barnwood*, *The Able Muse* and *Other Poetry*. His first collection was published in May 2008. A second followed in 2010. A third collection has been accepted for publication by Salmon Press.

Catherine Bruton was born in Warrington (back in the day when it was still in Lancashire!) and brought up in Lymm, Cheshire. She now lives near Bath with her husband and two small children, but she still feels like she's coming home when she smells the soap suds belching out of chimneys at Warrington Bank Quay Station. She works as a teacher and journalist, writing articles for *The Times* and the *Express* and a variety of magazines. She is also a successful novelist. Her next novel, *We Can be Heroes* will be published by Egmont in August 2011 and she is currently working on a new novel set in Warrington.

Robbie Burton runs Cross Border Poets, a Poetry Society Stanza that meets every month at Clwyd Theatr Cymru. Robbie spent most of her life in Warrington where she found inspiration for her poetry on the banks of the Manchester Ship Canal but since moving to Flintshire in 2008 she's been teetering on the edge of Hope Mountain instead. In 2003 Robbie gained an MA in Creative Arts: Reading and Writing Poetry and since then has been published in numerous magazines and anthologies. In 2009 she was shortlisted for the Poetry Business Pamphlet Competition.

Jake Campbell is from South Shields and has spent the past four years in Chester, where he has recently completed an MA in Creative Writing. Work completed on this course formed the basis for a collection of poetry in which the author takes the reader on a metaphysical journey from Sunderland to Newcastle, exploring the landscapes, memories and industrial vacillations that have shaped the region and his personal identity. His poem for *Still Life*, 'My Granddad Buries King at Souter Lighthouse', is part of this wider, lyrical investigation into the nature of place and belonging which he hopes to publish as a book in the near future. Living again in the North East, he continues to write and perform poetry and short stories, while he waits for the Grim-Reaper-esque figure of the fabled 'real world' to knock on his door and haul him to work, whenever or wherever that may be.

Helen Clare is an ex-science teacher, ex-literature development worker, ex-Arts Council Education Officer, and these days will do just about anything (that she can persuade anyone to pay her for) that involves creative writing, science and learning. She lives in Manchester but works all across the North West. At the moment she's working on a project that uses creative writing to help young people think about genetics. Her first collection *Mollusc* was published in 2004 by Comma Press and her poems have won a number of national prizes, including first prize in the London Writers' Competition 2002, and Runner Up in the *Daily Telegraph*/Arvon Competition,

2000. In 2007 she was Poet in Residence at the Museum of Science and Industry in Manchester. She's still slowly writing material for a second collection. When she's not doing that she's usually making corsets, fussing over her house rabbit or watching cricket.

John Davies was raised on the mean streets of Bromborough, where he remembers trails to the Ferry and to Raby Mere; Alley-o; daylong football matches; scrapes in the woods; hedge-hopping; apple-scrumping opportunities; and Guy Fawking outside the Merebrook. He emigrated to Liverpool to live above various pubs on Dale Street, and to fall in love with a girl who turned out to be the Sidhe-Queen. His studies at Manchester University included a stint as an apprentice gravedigger by way of a summer job. He is a member of the Poised Pen Writers of Bold Street, who run a fortnightly workshop providing support for the creatively adventurous and the bone idle. He has had work accepted by *Smoke*, *Nerve*, *The Interpreter's House*, *Weyfarers* and *Fire* magazines, and Big Pulp and Lightning Flash e-zines (US). For inspiration, he is drawn equally to Yeats, J.G. Ballard and Tom Waits.

Jennifer Anne Durban has fond memories of growing up in South Wales. She taught English in India for two years with Voluntary Service Overseas. After an enjoyable time studying with the Open University, she was awarded a postgraduate degree in 2001. Since retiring from teaching English and Drama in Cheshire schools, Jennifer has begun writing creatively, mainly poetry. She lives in Chester, enjoys theatre and music and has a nagging wish to return to India.

Heather Freckleton was brought up in Birmingham and has lived in many different places. Having been in Chester for eleven years now, she feels she is just beginning to settle. She has had numerous jobs including professional puppeteer, college lecturer and painter and decorator, but her most long-standing work has been as a social worker. She enjoys all kinds of writing and managed to get a short story in the Cheshire Prize anthology, *Zoo*, last year. Above all she especially enjoys writing poetry with which she has had some minor success. In between doing odd jobs and dreaming she continues to write ...

Simon Gotts was born and raised in Kent, but lived in Chester for nearly twenty years, until a recent move to Wales. He has won prizes for both short stories and poetry, including previous Cheshire Prize competitions. Many of his poems are narrative, as they have a tendency to form themselves quite quickly and then just need polishing. However, the polishing often takes years, including long periods spent in dank desk drawers.

Caroline Hawkridge's first women's health book stayed in print for eighteen years. After her last book for Penguin, Caroline turned to her love of poetry. She gained an MA in Creative Writing (distinction) from Manchester Metropolitan University (MMU) and was nominated for Faber New Poets. Her favourite poetry surprises have been publication in Carol Ann Duffy's 'Poetry Corner' in the *Daily Mirror* and having poems chosen by the Moorland Discovery Centre to celebrate bog plants. Caroline lives in Northwich and enjoys creative community projects. She has landed good press coverage for Poets & Players, Zest! and Fourpenny Circus. In 2008, she ran MMU's Words on Film festival and received the Janet Beer Prize. In the summer of 2010 she managed Simon Armitage's project to walk the Pennine Way as a modern troubadour. Imagine the fun of bartering everything needed for the 264 miles with communities en route – and all in return for poetry!

Angi Holden moved to Cheshire in the mid-seventies as a newly-qualified accountant, trained in 3D Design and – three children later – finally graduated in Creative Writing. Her poems and stories for both adults and children have been published in anthologies and magazines, ranging from *The Oxford Reading Tree* and *The Poetry Store* to the University of Chester's *Flash* and MMU's *Muse*. She is now an Associate Lecturer in the Department of Contemporary Arts at MMU Cheshire

Barbara Holliday grew up in Ellesmere Port and discovered a love of creative writing at infant school. She still has a copy of her first illustrated story, *Super Cat*, written at the age of six. A love of English and Drama throughout her education led to a degree in English Literature and Creative Writing from Manchester Metropolitan University in 1993. The need for a 'day job' begrudgingly led her to take an admin course, but she soon discovered that she rather liked it and has worked in administration ever since, including a ten-year stint at Chester Gateway Theatre as PA to the Chief Executive and Directors. She now works as a Research Administrator in the Faculty of Health and Social Care at the University of Chester, is a wife and mother, and in her spare time likes to write, research her family history and bake cakes.

George Horsman has had numerous poems published and a range of short stories published or broadcast as well as having co-authored a novel. He has won regional awards for his work and has had a play performed locally. Now retired from academic life, he lives in Chester and, while devoting most of his energies to writing and to choral and orchestral music, he finds time to learn Spanish and to walk the Welsh hills.

Linda Houlton works in Chester and lives on the Wirral in a house which some would choose for its panoramic views of the Liverpool skyline, but which Linda chose for its proximity to her local pub. She is currently working on a poetry anthology, *Of All the Gin Joints,* based on various bars she has experienced on her travels and is enjoying the research. A long-standing and enthusiastic member of the University of Liverpool Creative Writing Society, she is the judge of their Annual International Ted Walters writing competition, now in its fifth year. Linda has had poems published in various anthologies and publications and has broadcast her poetry on local television and radio. She has performed her work in small theatres and venues around Wirral and Liverpool. She also works as a restaurant critic.

Peter Howard lives in Warrington, works in Manchester and holidays wherever he can. A technical writer by profession, he sometimes escapes the straitjackets of standards and specifications to write poetry and short stories. A stop-start creative writing career has been underscored by the odd mention in dispatches, here and there; but nothing to write home about. He's delighted to be published again and promises to try harder. Now 'on the back nine,' he is happily surrounded by his growing family and the Sunday supplements.

Richard Hughes was born and brought up in Seven Sisters, South Wales. He read English at Swansea University and gained a postgraduate teaching qualification at Cheltenham. He has worked as a researcher with the BBC, a librarian with Ilford Ltd, and for five years tried to sell second-hand books. However, most of his working life has been spent teaching English in South Manchester. In recent years he has had poems published in *Other Poetry*, *The Interpreter's House* and *Orbis*.

Alison Leonard was raised a Yorkshire-woman but has spent most of her adult life in Chester. Writing was her first love: she had a poem published at eleven and wrote a play when she was sixteen. Getting into print had to wait till she was nearly thirty, because wanting to earn a living and start a family got in the way. Life – including volunteer work for the Quakers and the Green movement – has continued to get happily in the way, but her list of publications ranges from fiction for young people and plays for youth theatre, to drama and short stories for BBC radio and poetry in local and national anthologies. She recently gained an MA with distinction from Manchester Metropolitan University with a novel that brings to life a woman who modelled for Edgar Degas; a group from this MA are planning a new venture in audio-book publishing.

Vikki Littlemore is an undergraduate at the University of Chester, studying English and Creative Writing.

Ellis Lloyd is not this person's real name. If you were this person you would have been born a Welsh Liverpudlian, had Greek and Latin thrust upon you, and would have achieved a smattering of history and philosophy. Then you would escape the classics to spend a working life in finance and economics, crafting deathless technocratic prose. This dismal progress would be happily relieved by marriage and children; also by an acting itch when young and foolish, a singing itch throughout life and a writing itch in the last dozen years of a long retirement (when old and foolish). Ellis (a Cheshire resident for over forty years) is driven to enter competitions by a thirst for valid criticism, and is humbly grateful when the criticism takes the form of a short-listing or a designation as runner-up.

Liz Loxley grew up near Bristol and moved to Cheshire in 2000. She now lives in Flintshire with her civil partner, Helen and their three lovely cats. Liz and Helen are both members of Chester Poets, through which they met, and of ID Books. Liz is now studying for an MA in Creative Writing (Poetry) at Manchester Metropolitan University. Her poems have been anthologised by publishers including Faber, Penguin and Oxford University Press, have appeared in various poetry magazines and been studied by school students. She has won, been placed and been shortlisted in a number of poetry competitions.

Anna Mackenzie comes from the depths of the Ribble Valley in Lancashire; she studied English Literature at the University of Chester, graduating in 2008, and then defected to Liverpool for a Masters in Renaissance and Eighteenth-Century Literature. She returned to Chester in 2009 to pursue a PhD focusing on Shakespeare, and currently works in the English Department as a Visiting Lecturer. She has had poems published in various poetry magazines, including *Albatross*, *Anon*, and *Krax*. Anna is Associate Editor for 'The Shakespeare Standard,' she also co-hosts inked, a creative-writing open mic night in Chester. One New Year's resolution for 2011 is to start writing poetry on a regular basis again, as she has neglected it horrendously. Long-term ambitions include: becoming a legitimate 'Shakespearean;' hugging Ian McKellen; and being Bernard from *Black Books* on evenings and weekends.

Clive McWilliam has worked throughout Britain and abroad as a Landscape Architect and Illustrator and has his own practice in Chester. In 2010 he was highly commended for the Forward Prize for Best Single Poem and was short listed for the Manchester Prize. In the same year he won second prize in both the Poetry London Competition and The Troubadour International. In 2008 he came first in the Virginia Warbey Poetry Prize and third in The National Poetry Competition. Clive's work has appeared in *The Rialto*, *Magma*, *Poetry London* and *Poetry Review* and he has recently read with Carol Ann Duffy and friends at the Royal Exchange Theatre in Manchester.

Russell Morris is a painter, sculptor and teacher currently based at Victoria Mill Arts in Congleton, Cheshire. The creative dialogue between visual art and poetry lies at the heart of his work as a fine artist and has formed the basis for two recent collaborative exhibitions with poets drawn from the Cheshire region.

Jonathan Musgrove spent his childhood in the fresh country air of Moor End, Mellor: happy memories of toboggan rides in the winter and warm sunny days of hide-and-seek in the summer. A graduate in engineering from the University of Liverpool he later researched for a Masters in Theology at Chester. He now runs a commercial consultancy in the engineering, construction and rail industries. He thought his poetry was a recent phenomenon but has now rediscovered lines he wrote while working in the Middle East in the 70s. He finds inspiration everywhere and in every person and event he encounters, but is perhaps most inspired by his creative family and when walking in the Clwydian Range. Every so often further scribblings are gathered up and added to a green expanding folder.

Jean Page was born in Liverpool. She was educated at the University of Liverpool, and is a recent postgraduate of the University of Chester. A teacher for fourteen years, she is the mother of a grown up son. Her poetry has featured on Radio Merseyside's *Art Waves* programme; her plays have received rehearsed readings at the Pyramid Arts Centre Warrington and the Gateway Theatre Chester. She was included in the short list for the Sefton Literary Festival poetry prize, and long-listed for North West Playwrights' *Striking Silver* competition. Her prose fiction has appeared in the University of Chester's *Flash* Magazine. Home is a small cottage at the foot of a hill in Frodsham, shared with family, friends, and books.

James Phillips was born and raised in Wallasey. He has taught English in a Cheshire secondary school for the last decade. James has written a couple of plays, a few short stories, a screenplay and other bits of literary fluff. He hates writing 'biogs' because he is then faced with the uncomfortable truth that, to the rest of the world at least, he is an incurable dilettante. James does not consider himself to be, in Auden's words, one of the 'over-earnest people' (i.e. a bore) but he does, when writing, at least, worry about 'the eternal verities' – a tendency W.H. thought infra dig. No kids. No cats.

Sheila Powell was born in Wales and attended Grove Park Grammar School. After four years in a Path. Lab. she went to California and took care of horses and children. College followed, with three years spent teaching English at Christleton High School in Chester. She has raised two sons and now has three adorable granddaughters. She still teaches privately and works part-time in the local school and community library. In her spare time she enjoys walking, gardening and writing. Her real love is writing for children and it is her ambition to see one of her children's stories illustrated and in print.

Rita Ray lives in Lymm, Cheshire. She divides her time between art and writing and exhibits paintings with a local society, her speciality being portraits. She finds looking closely at a person to paint a portrait feels much like composing a poem. She also finds art a rich source of ideas for poems. Travel sharpens perceptions of the world. In particular, two trips to China, working on an education project based in Lanzhou, inspired some of Rita's poems. Her poetry has been published in several journals, including *TLS* and *PEN Review*. She has also published poetry and stories for children.

Jonny Reid was born in Belfast in 1984. His work has appeared, and is forthcoming, in magazines such as *The Hat, London Grip, Magma, Stand, Stride* and *The Warwick Review*. He is currently studying for an MA in Creative Writing at the University of Manchester and works in a youth centre. He was raised in Newcastle-under-Lyme and attended Alsager Comprehensive and has been long-listed twice for an Eric Gregory award.

Emma Rees (Editor, and Chair, Judging Panel) is Senior Lecturer at the University of Chester. Her first book was *Margaret Cavendish* and she is currently working on her second, *Can't: Revealing the Vagina in Literature and the Arts*. She has contributed essays to four recent books: *Rhetorics of Bodily Disease and Health in Medieval and Early Modern England*; *The Female Body in Medicine and Literature*; *Studying Literature*; and *Led Zeppelin and Philosophy*. In 2010 she edited the Cheshire Prize short-story anthology, *Zoo*. Emma was born and bred in Birmingham, moving to Chester in 1999 after living in Norwich for several years, where she taught at UEA. She spends any spare time she has with her husband, daughter, four cats and dog at home in Handbridge. She spends any spare cash she has on going to rock concerts, the theatre and the cinema; buying books and stationery; and on running a tremendously impractical but beautiful car.

Frances Sackett was born in Wales but has lived in the North West for over thirty years. Frances has been published in numerous UK magazines and journals and has contributed to anthologies on the Brontës, railways, parents, childhood and others. Her collection of poems *The Hand Glass* is published by Seren. Jobs have included working in a bank, bringing up two daughters and, latterly, working in a bookshop and tutoring poetry in Manchester for CCE. She is now retired. Her poems have also appeared in the previous Cheshire Prize anthologies *Elements* and *Life Lines*.

Michael Scully has been trying to write poetry since he was a child. His very first poem, written when he was about seven or eight, was part of a school English lesson and was about Father Christmas. For the 2010 Cheshire Prize competition he submitted three poems (written many, many years later) that centre on his childhood relationship with his father. In the era when he was growing up, fathers were not generally demonstrative towards their sons and he does not recall his father ever being so with him. It was not until he was an adult himself that he understood just how deep his father's affection for him was. He now views his father as a very strong and capable man who taught him many practical things.

David Selzer was born in London in 1942. He is a published poet, winner of the Eric Gregory Award and the Felicia Hemans Prize. He has been writing poetry for more than half a century. Since leaving Cheshire County Council in 2001, after thirty years plus working in education, first as a teacher and then an adviser, in addition to continuing to write poems, he has completed four screenplays, two stage plays (for one of which he was a finalist in the Sussex Playwrights Club 2009 full length play competition) and set up a website – www.davidselzer.com – to publish his work. He is also chair of Action Transport Theatre, a professional theatre company based in Ellesmere Port, specialising in work for, with and by, children and young people.

Ruth A. Symes grew up in Warrington (a town of 'wire and water'), spent several years in the South and in York and currently lives in Altrincham. After an early career in academia and in editing, she is now a freelance writer and historian working mainly for family history magazines such as *Who Do You Think You Are?* and *Family Tree Magazine*. She has published a number of academic books together with a book on family history: *Stories from Your Family Tree: Ancestors Within Living Memory* (The History Press, 2009). Ruth now has a young daughter, Ruby, and writing is taking second place – for a while.

Angela Topping writes poetry for both adults and children. She is a full-time freelance writer and poet-in-schools. She is the author of four solo collections, the most recent being *The New Generation*, published by Salt (2010). In 2011, three chapbooks are out: *I Sing of Bricks* (Salt); *Catching On*, an elegiac sequence for Matt Simpson (Rack Press); and *The Lightfoot Letters* (Erbacce). This last volume accompanies an exhibition of artwork by Maria Walker at The Brindley, based on the discovery of some family letters from 1923. Angela recently read at The Poetry Cafe at The Poetry Society in London, and has also performed across the North West in libraries and other venues. She also writes critical books and textbooks on literary texts for OUP and Greenwich Exchange, following 16 years as a teacher in Cheshire.

Judy Ugonna studied at Trinity College Dublin and then did a postgraduate diploma in librarianship in London. After doing VSO and working in Africa for twenty years, Judy worked internationally for the British Council, and was awarded the OBE for her information work with the British Council in 2005. Judy started Poem Catchers (www.poemcatchers.com) with poet Gill McEvoy to provide affordable poetry writing workshops in the Chester and Wirral environs. She is part of Chester's Zest! Open Floor Poetry Night management team and a member of the Poem Shed, a writing collective, also based in Chester. Nearer to home, she runs a small poetry writing group called Poets à Hoy in Hoylake. Judy also participates in and helps to run various other community arts events and programmes in the Wirral, for example the Wirral Open Studio Tour 2010, and the Wirral Community Choir. Judy has four grown-up sons and four young grandchildren.

Philip Watts was born in Sale, Cheshire and, after teaching English in London for half of his life, returned to his native county ten years ago. He lives in Holmes Chapel and follows a portfolio career including tutoring, acting as Interpreter Guide at Tatton Park and working in his local library. He has read his work at the Manchester Poetry Festival and the Knutsford Literature Festival and for several years ran Outwrite, a Manchester-based writing group to support the LGBT community. He has a poem published in *Homage to Cheshire*, the anthology compiled by the last Cheshire Poet Laureate.

Philip Williams was born and grew up in South Wales and briefly emigrated with his parents and twin brother to Australia as a 'Ten Pound Pom'. He developed his love of poetry at a 'bog-standard comprehensive' with extraordinary teachers and visits from Gillian Clarke, Dannie Abse and other luminaries. He studied at the University of Leeds and worked in marketing and PR, with management roles at Huddersfield and Keele Universities. He is now freelance, lives with his wife and teenage daughters in Alsager and belongs to the Congleton Writers' Forum and the Poetry Society's Stoke Stanza.

Joy Winkler was born in Barnsley but has lived 'this side' of the Pennines for twenty-three years. She was Cheshire Poet Laureate in 2005 and subsequently toured with former Laureate colleagues as Bunch of Fives and Fourpenny Circus, delivering innovative poetry performance across the North West and Midlands. Joy's work has been published in various magazines and has had success in several competitions. She has had three collections of poetry published, including, most recently, *On the Edge*. Her work often draws on the detail of everyday life in both its poignancy and its humour. Joy facilitates a number of workshops and projects in the North West, working with community groups in the Salford and Rochdale areas. She was writer in residence in HMP Styal for seven years and now works as part of the Writers in Prison Network.

FOREWORD

> We are the you and I who were
> They whom we remember.
> Wendell Berry

We never read the same poem twice. Each time we come to it we have changed and our interaction with it is altered too. Sometimes such changes might be scarcely perceptible, but they are there nonetheless, informing and reframing our interpretation in a myriad of ways. This potential we have – and that a poem has – is one of the reasons why a poetry anthology can be a source of almost endless pleasure. In Berry's lines the 'we,' 'you,' 'I,' and 'they' are not fixed but are endlessly reimagined by the poet and by his readers, too. Like Gormley's statues on Crosby Sands, a poem is only truly 'alive' in the act of being observed. When given a voice, the iron men speak (as Ellis Lloyd so vividly imagines in this anthology). They become intermediaries between humanity and nature – created by the one and little by little returning to the other. What they leave behind is literally nothing but, paradoxically, everything.

This idea of heredity and legacy preoccupies many of the anthology's contributors. Some of the poems play with ideas of memory; others use old photographs – the still lives of the modern era – to prompt recollection: that which has lain trapped between the pages of a book or a photo album, or which has simply been lost in the hectic whirl of someone's past, can breathe again in poetry. Many of the anthology's poems use familiar images to attempt to answer – or at least to establish – the 'big' questions of life: where have we come from and where are we going? As the nineteenth-century poet Thomas Campbell suggested, 'To live in hearts we leave behind is not to die,' and poetry certainly offers one form of immortality. In his exquisitely knotty lines, then, Berry suggests something about memory: there's a 'still life' that is recalled and the very act of recollection endows it with a vitality and *movement* which makes it powerful. When Wordsworth wrote about poetry as 'emotion recollected in tranquillity' he wasn't suggesting in 'tranquillity' some kind of stasis but, rather, an 'overflow of powerful feelings,' an activity of creative energy.

Given poetry's complex relationship with memory, then, it comes as little surprise that so many of this anthology's poets return to childhood for their subject matter. Childhoods are sometimes fondly recalled, but can also be a source of pain. Mysteries are still all around and adult poets revisit their origins in an attempt to revive mystery and to *still* regrets so that the ordinariness of life may be less painfully resumed. As Tolstoy wrote at the start of *Anna Karenina*, 'Happy families are all alike; every unhappy family is unhappy in its own way,' and those 'ways' are explored in these pages.

Still Life is a rich and textured collection of poems. The best among them transfigure the ordinary so that music stands become 'corvine' (crow-like) and, in the stifling closeness of a summer garden, 'Dragons dart / In flight.' Some of the poems experiment with form and structure – the Haiku and sonnet are favourites – but that experimentation is more an imaginative rejuvenation of, than a slavish adherence to, those forms. As the lines I have quoted already suggest, nature plays a key role in many of the poems. Birds feature frequently and this in itself is suggestive of how poetry can immortalise something fleeting and short-lived: dead or alive, common or rare, birds leave an enduring impression on many of the speakers of these poems.

But all is not sombre: the anthology's humorous contributions, too, can challenge our preconceptions. An object as mundane as a cheeseboard may, in a skilled poet's hand, be transformed into a sensual, erotic space of exploration and fulfilment (see Linda Houlton's contribution). Any successful poem, be it light-hearted or serious, will leave a trace on its reader like the retinal stain from a camera flash or, as Clive McWilliam expresses it in this volume, a 'spot-weld behind' our eyes. Every poem in this anthology is 'successful,' of course, for one reason or another, but there were four contributions that were judged to have exceptional merit. The overall winner of the 2010 Prize was Rita Ray for her beautiful, contemplative 'Still Life With Oranges and Walnuts (Luis Meléndez).' Helen Clare won second prize for her '*Gerris lacustris*, Common Pond Skater;' Simon Gotts came third with 'The Careers Master;' and Clive McWilliam was commended for his poem 'Spellbound.'

I would like to thank my colleagues on the judging panel: Peter Blair, Francesca Haig and John Scrivener. I would also like to thank the poet Simon Armitage for gamely reading out the winning entries at the awards evening in October 2010, and the High Sheriff of Cheshire, Diana Barbour, for announcing the winners' names and presenting them with their prizes. Lynda Baguley and Jenni Westcott of the University of Chester's Corporate Communications office have maintained their formidable reputations as outstanding organisers and administrators at every point in the Prize process. Sarah Griffiths has been a wonderfully efficient editor for the

University of Chester Press: her patience made my life a lot easier as I tried to juggle teaching and researching with the editing of this volume. I am also grateful for the help of Derek Alsop, Graham Atkin, Matt Davies, Melissa Fegan, Sarah Heaton, Yvonne Siddle, William Stephenson, Alan Wall, Chris Walsh, Sally West and Richard E. Wilson. Thanks are due too to Bank of America: at a time when central funding for the arts is under attack, the Bank's continued support is both remarkable and reassuring.

Emma Rees
Chair, Judging Panel, and Editor, *Still Life*
Department of English
University of Chester
18 February 2011

STILL LIFE WITH ORANGES AND WALNUTS
(LUIS MELÉNDEZ)

Rita Ray

First I notice the pumpkin – or is it a melon?
Did they have melons?

It must be late afternoon as the light slants in
making plain wood boxes shine like ingots.
They will eat the shelled walnuts after dinner.

An orange is set apart – for balance,
to fill a too-empty space.

In the manner of the old masters the canvas
was prepared with rich raw sienna
that glows through fruit skins and terra cotta.

One by one the oranges will disappear
to be peeled, squeezed, sucked.

The little boys turning the spit
will open their eyes in wonder,
hope to scoop a fingerful of juice
from the scrubbed-out well in the table.

I want to believe there are cooks
and maids, hot in mob caps,
fetching and peeling,
calling, 'Hurry, hurry!'

But there is no kitchen,
no boys turning the spit
and dreaming of oranges,

only a fiction of angles and shadows
secret codes to fool the eye, to lie to us –
the covered jug, the fruit forever ripe.

The dark backboard ends at the frame's edge.
You are alone in that small space
wiping your brushes on a rag

for the light is going
and you have no way of keeping it.

DIPTYCH

Philip Williams

'As for the appeal of icons to popular sentiment, perhaps this was best understood by local Soviet commanders in the 1930s […] ordered to campaign against the influence of the Church, they were known to line up icons, sentence them to death and then shoot them.'

Judith Herrin, *Byzantium*

A stern Christ, a Theotokos, wise
and almond-eyed, the cloud of painted
witnesses who watched the priest,
week by week, bustling and fussing
behind the iconostasis,
each time observed, in spoon and chalice
the invisible, miraculous change.

Windows to heaven, dismantled, dislodged,
stacked in a shuttered row against the wall.

At the reading of the charges, the charging
of the barrels, the belt-feed, bolt-click, taking aim,
many wept. And, in the stillness before
the splintering dance of painted panels
disintegrating in an iron wind,
and in the stillness beyond, the steady
crossing and recrossing of fingers,
dipping and rising like the dipping and rising
of the golden spoon.

THE CUPBOARD UNDER THE STAIRS

Jennifer Anne Durban

One ... two ... three ... four ...
Inch open the door,
bowelling guardian of dark disguise
offer up your secrets.
Feather-light mackintosh,
cradling last summer's sand dunes, mother of pearl,
mackerel memory, Cornish ices, clotted cream.
Faded striped beach-bag shielding swimsuits
woollen to bikini-string
tanging salt of many seas.

Five ... six ... seven ...
Discarded coats, hats, scarves coiled,
Wellington boots, black, size-ranged, paired
conjuring long-remembered
sledging, sliding, gathering holly.
Gut-strung tennis racquets, splintered hockey sticks
fix perpetual first reserve, eclipse team dream;
scant-haired violin bows suspended,
hooks assertive as chapel hat-pegs,
proclaim music's precedence
over rank shoe-bag, ball cornucopia, ping pong to beach.

Eight ... Nine ...
Sturdy shoe-box tucks
black and tan shoe-polish, suede brush, heel grips,
insoles, acrid plimsoll whitener.
In deep shadow-space,
reverse staircase encountering hall floor,
pastoral living-room pictures deposed,
protect doll's house, thread-stripped Teddy, spineless
Bambi, *Heidi*, *Noddy*, *Rupert Bear*.

Ten …
Coming, ready or not.

Found you!
Child asleep
pitch womb hedgehogged
among detritus, experience, age.
Must I prise you out?

HIDE AND SEEK

Heather Freckleton

The seeker's looking
but might not risk the
forbidden stairs to the attic
where you stumble behind
bags and boxes sagged in desolation
and imagine the bitter scold
of the music stand,
leant corvine, in the corner.

Smiling, you sit in gritty dust
that clings to your touch,
foot tapping a rigid thing and it's there;
lying like a creature's innards,
pond eyes alive with the electric light.
A gas mask; coiled lung-spine
drawn down to a tin of rusted breath
held for sixty years.

You don't want to but you see it rise;
hollow eyes drawing you in
chaos scratching in the dust
by the deadened weight of tin,
rattle breath snagging your ears
as it nears, its dark cheeks
flapping like charred skin.

And your fear has you cat skim
down the stairs ignoring
the hideous twist of a long dead

spider in your hair and you hide
behind a wardrobe door where

only the blouses breathe.

HAIKU MOMENTS

Sheila Powell

Butterfly wing-beats
Strumming on tachyons of light,
Eternity's song

Skeins of silver mist
Unravel, weaving nets to
Catch the waking light

Filigree web-site –
Spider, not computer boffin
Soul information

FURNITURE COMPLEX

Anna Mackenzie

Fading in pastels:
guest-room shades remove life. I
apply foundation

to pale out tear marks.
The uneven carpet shakes:
too much brushed beneath.

WORMS

George Horsman

In the warm dark of their atrium they cling
to the crevice round the bin's lip and on its walls,
climbers whose body-tubes are all
they have for ropes. When I tilt
the lid they fall apart and hang
in rags like some shredded church banner or the silk

of a once-sexy undergarment fallen to tatters.
There's something snooty – or in flight? – about
the way they glue themselves above
the sludge they make and feed on – black potatoes,
the tang of grass cuttings, orange rind, the grout
of mulched-up carrots – as if they plot to move,

at risk of a cliff-face fall, clear of the mess.
something sly-sexual, too: the way they sometimes
zip up and hide, then slide out again, as if,
multitudinous, they're indifferent that you've guessed
their fertilising aim, a thousand entwined
pink infant-penises bent on renewing life.

SPELLBOUND

Clive McWilliam

Whoever sees the Kingfisher
returns besotted and changed,
will haunt the same brook for days
craving its tin-foil shock.

My first one left a leaf and water
spot-weld behind my eyes –
I throw sugar on the fire
to recreate its spark.

Saw you in a swoon in the stables last night
talking electric blue with the nag,
your tinsel stare told me
you had cut loose forever.

ADA IN THE GARDEN

Clive McWilliam

Ada in the garden
wears the time lapse veil
of a moth in flight.
She's as bright
as a cooling pond at dusk.

The moth eyed Ada
coming down from the grove
with the light of one who's seen
where the sun goes
when it leaves the hill.

And here's a photo –
a single breath in Ada's life
when a moth came
to dance round her face
before the night could claim it.

BURNING THE CLOTHES

Frances Sackett

'Burning the Clothes' and 'Shoreline' are the final poems of a sequence entitled Burning the Clothes *in memory of Andrew (July 1978– April 2005).*

'The artist is extremely lucky who is presented with the worst possible ordeal which will not kill him. At that point, he's in business.'

John Berryman

On sudden impulse
he went to the car –
took out black bags
that had been there for weeks;

the clothes that the police
had returned: designer shirts,
jeans, quirky caps, shoes
he had bought for his son.

The trees were the first to burn,
a mingling of pine and old apple,
their essence filling the garden,
then the wood and the clothes

burning together, flickering
and dropping their ash:
the trees he had climbed

as a child, now felled
for a view of the hills –
the healing dawn light.

SHORELINE

Frances Sackett

A stillness wraps you round,
warmth seeps into your bones,
the last cicada is running out of persistence
and the huge ocean
tells you to turn for home.

There are still moments to cherish,
voices that insist on meanings,
although the earth is weary of being questioned.

TWELVE MEN AND A CHEESEBOARD

Linda Houlton

Last night I had a Wensleydale with cranberries,
An architect with the soul of an artist,
he dressed buildings
with scarlet ribbons and gauze
but undressed me
indifferently.
A flaunting, flamboyant jester,
he made me yearn for

the Double Gloucester
consumed with sweet fervour and dry cider
on rolling Cotswold hills,

or the silent satisfaction
of my Ploughman's lunch.
A hunk of cheddar, a brick of bread,
a tankard of ale,
the scent of sun and straw.

Once, I crossed the Brecon Beacons,
sampled the twin tastes of Caerphilly.
The young was fresh and supple,
the Mature, more rounded at the edges.
They faded with the whisper of commitment.
Colloquially, they were the Crumblies.
I should choose an accountant,
safe and punctilious,
Stilton and port wine.
Yes, I could recline in red Chesterfield comfort,
if I could just bear the silence.

Perhaps Latin – a sprinkling of Parmesan,
the fizz of Prosecco
or a man sized Manchego,
heritage of Jerez, a light Fino.
I suspect they would be neglectful Narcissus
and I would pine
for lack of attention.

Not for me the blandness of a Dutch Edam
or the emptiness of Emmental.

Once, an imposter Camembert
tricked me into
the illusion of perfection.
A rare sophistication,
he proved to be as delicate
as Chablis.

And yes, I've had my share of
limp roulades
but still I dream.
The touch of velvet,
the bounty of kings,
the romance of Charlemagne.

And thus I pray:
Dear Lord, please send
maturity and melting passion,
the champagne of cheeses,
the best of men.
Next time, deliver unto me
the Brie.

THREADS

James Phillips

I. Morning

Sympathy.
When at play
one's horizon
is three feet
not three miles away.

Fantasia.
Beguiled by views,
long and slow,
plundering nature's undertow:
a fat leaf binds a chrysalis,
starlings fledge in garage eaves,
spiders weave in badly-pointed brick.

Synaesthesia:
a cluster of lavender is almost
conjured from hints of floral fabric softener;
a thrumming bee, preoccupied,
feels much warmer than fox fur;
words are textured, kept in attics,
wrapped in dust and soot;
bright insects make both mulch and music
beneath a tiny tyrant's foot.

Hypomania;
separate strands
begin to coalesce:
Surely some revelation is at hand?
Even at one's fingertips,
yea, and under one's nose,
and in one's close-

to-comprehending ear
the throbbing,
stinking Earth's
soliloquy is building.

Nearly nirvana:
but one does not
note the lappet
on one's pullover

unravelling.

II. Noon
All things must pass.

Some see scrolled lily pads
on ink-blot ponds,
bronzed Buddleia heads
lolling over sepia grass, soil
stretching under those nettle beds:

never Narcissus in T-shirt and slacks.

On the lawn of a cool walled garden
his likeness reclines in the shade,
ignorant of the varicose sun
bleeding light – blinding and strange.

Reflection, like knitwear, redundant.

III. Post Meridian
One vast recumbent afternoon
when promises of heat have gone,
an occidental glance is met
with crippling glint of dying sun.

We know we shan't look up again
in these dire diurnal silences,
but sleep in fraying cardigans
and glower at moons.

THE CAREERS MASTER

Simon Gotts

I followed him in
to what was little more
than a closet.
Two steel cabinets
a table
two plywood chairs
a waste bin
an Anglepoise lamp
and a coat-stand
regarded us coldly
like the occupants
of a crowded lift
in the summer sales.

He sat,
tugged his trousers
over his knees
to avoid stretching
the weave,
cracked his fingers,
steepled them
in front of his beak.

*It's all a question of which field
you wish to enter.*

I should have said
The field where
stiff green shoots
stalk the winter plough,
where southern breezes
comb ryegrass over the hill's brow,

where hares start up and bound
at the spill of my shadow, and
swallows suture the engorged air
above the bleaching barley.
The field where flaxen girls go
to ripen their heads to gold, and
commit acts of reckless generosity.

I should have said
The field where the artist
sits at a clean canvas
contemplating fat crows,
where a writer swats away the punctuation
that settles on his prose,
where the philosopher slants
a pale straw hat over his rubicund
nose, and leans back on his lover's
sun-bathed breast.
The field where all dreams are made flesh,
all grass is made hay;
the field whose gate is wide open.

GRASSHOPPER GIRL

Jean Page

Lara flies in from the East
Our Grasshopper girl
Newly sprung from a dusty, rusting, rickshaw
Yen on her palms
Lotus flower face
Amber-studded eyes set in a small skull,
A garland of seed pearl teeth beneath,
Strung out in a smile.
She settles on my arm, her voice whirrs.

COTTON ATLAS

Jean Page

A sunset on a sun-dress
Rouge raspberries, streaked, stuffed
Into yellow-piped pockets
Embroidered on the outside with white stitched daffodils.
A spreading map of the world
A flapping cotton atlas, dripping dark purple islands
Whole continents emerging,
A geography of juice.
Previously pristine, a miniature colossus with plaits
Presiding, now painted, pagan.
Antarctica a blob of ice-cream;
America just a stain.

PAPER PATTERNS

Angela Topping

Make me a dress the colour of sky
just after a June sunset, or one
like that velvet in George Henry Lee's
expensive Christmas window.

God love her, she'd try. Her mouth
prickled with a metal smile of pins
as she unrolled market-stall cloth,
spread crackling paper patterns.

She'd labour on at her Singer,
her small feet dancing the two-step
on the treadle, tunelessly humming,
secure in motherly skills.

But I failed to measure up, came to
dread her home-sewn lumpy seams,
gave up romance, took to wearing
lumberjack shirts, cut-down jeans.

MOON WALK

Frances Sackett

The hospital silent at night,
padding the corridors, heavy with milk,
I watch white, swirling images on the screen.

Men walking on the moon!
And you born into this new world.
Tiny fingers curl around mine,

your body still holding its foetus shape,
I watch topsy-turvy swirling,
milky with vapour and moonscape.

This ward, this night flowing with exploration.
Beginnings. Love coming into being –
As you open your eyes and we

look at each other, inside those pools
depths never charted before, newer
than space discovery,

newer than infinite astronomy.

AMARYLLIS

Philip Watts

I was given the plant at Christmas
And didn't get around to getting it going,
So that when I finally opened the box,
Well into the year, I found with distaste
That it had taken the lead
And in its dark little cell
Had produced a withered shoot and half-flower –
An etiolated foetus, an abortion
Of the bloom it was supposed to be.

Not deterred by this sickening stillbirth,
Heartened by the reassurance on the carton,
I removed the alien head
And set about putting things to rights:
Bedding the bulb in its container,
With compost, moisture and care
In appropriate proportions.

And, surely enough, the promised rebirth occurred –
The shoots second-chanced it through the earth;
And now a solid green mast supports
Huge loudspeaker blooms which face the sun,
Trumpeting optimism in scarlet and white,
Announcing: you can begin again;
You can get it right.

EARLY SPARROW-GRASS

Liz Loxley

The asparagus season came early
that year. We were playing house, with mother
away. I took a tight band of brothers,
placed them tenderly knee-deep in water
where they stood to attention, their spears
pointing upwards like fingers of two hands.
I poked their stalks with a knife, the tip sank
in with a little resistance; their green
had softened. We rolled their heads in butter,
nibbled them as grease dripped down our fingers.
Later, the fetid smell in our urine,
my inheritance. Your last asparagus.

PONTOON

Liz Loxley

Our game was conceived in DNA:
your not being the father I wanted,
my not being your choice of daughter.

We used a card table, before its relegation
to the garden shed. Imagine us seated
at that table: grazed green baize of its surface,
a pack of cards with fraying edges.

Neither of us willing to concede or trust;
and so – twist, twist, twist, twist
till we both were bust.

SLOE GIN

Liz Loxley

After the first frost he would take his walking stick
and hook down branches of blackthorn to pick the sloes;
tongue clamped between teeth, he'd prick their skins, and pop them
in a jar, add some sugar, then top up with gin.
As autumn turned to winter, the sealed jar would sit
on a shelf in the cool and dark of the garage,
only disturbed to be turned and turned again, till
it was Christmas week and the time for decanting.
That drink took pride of place among bottles on top
of the piano: liquor the colour of blood.
Now I hook branches of the past, capture the taste
of each fresh mouthful, how it bit one's tongue, like love,
and marvel at how those sloes were transformed – who would
have thought it: something so bitter, tempered by time.

DARWIN'S FINCHES

Rob Blaney

Reptiles gather to worship the sun, sailors break fragrant sticks
from incense trees to light beacons.

Distracted with waiting, men patch together threadbare songs,
carve their names on the cliff and wait for breeze to shift the
        doldrums.

Subdued after three years of absence, he climbs the volcano,
a moonscape of pyramids older than Genesis,
makes numerous stops at dust summits on the winding path to
        the salt-crust lake
where he stoops, swallows from thirst, watches feral goats drink
        brine
without burning their throats.

He follows a rash of cactus finches as they tumble through the
        Caldera
and roost on parched trees to drill into rock seed with their bills.
In the shape of their beaks is the secret of evolution,
the solution to a puzzle he toils to solve.

At dusk, as he listens to the groan of the sea, answers still evade
        him;
It is like grasping the gist of a new language,
seeing a starburst from a ship for the first time.
He sits on the beach by the campfire, sketches silhouettes and as he
        ponders
the enormity of his reasoning,
Iguanas perched on magma cliffs spit clouds of salt to mock him.

THE MIGRANT

Angi Holden

The boy cradles the limp bird, a prayer draped
across his palms. Its head swings back,
the neck slumped and flaccid. Feathers
spring apart, exposing shaft and vane,
pale and scrawny flesh. He burrows stubby fingers
into velvet plumage, discovers shades of chocolate,
of russet, copper, gold, fanned across his broken nails.
He smoothes the plush of ruffled breast,
spreads the broken wing.

A rare Bean Goose, a juvenile, his father says.
Like him, an exile from the harsh and hungry cold,
a wanderer, in search of food and sanctuary.
A first migration, now its last.

The child looks up, sees in this man a youth
displaced, forced into leaving home. His flight sudden;
his route uncertain; his journey crossing borders,
checkpoints, boundaries. His tentative arrival
in these bleak and lonely fens he now calls home.

Later, crouched on kitchen flags blooming with down,
fat spitting from the blackened tray,
the boy explores the bird's abandoned crop.
Finds hidden in the gizzard
a lode of pebbles from a distant land.

ROOK AND JACKDAW MIGRATIONS OBSERVED IN GERMANY 1942–1945

Richard Hughes

During World War II John Buxton, Peter Conder and George Waterston co-opted fellow prisoners of war to count birds, especially rooks, flying over their camps. In 1949 their findings were published as a paper.

    I.   Officer
Three of them: Buxton, Conder, Waterston.
Officers like the rest of us. Duties
paralysed. Pestered by shame. Or relief.
Fastened to a patch of land. Dössell camp.
Watched by hostile wire and black pine deepening
to Warburgh beyond hopeless horizons.

Yes, three of them. One day, inspection done,
they spoke up. A plan. Asked for volunteers.
'What, counting bloody birds?' someone muttered.
Felt the same myself. But I did it.
We all did. Took our places on the dawn to dusk
shift. Keeping birds' hours, I suppose.

    II.   Buxton
Right. Rooks. The autumn westward flight for warmth
returns in spring. Flocks. Rarely fewer than three.
Be sharp. Study these silhouettes. Observe
the wheatsheaf tail, curved claw-toothed wings, noble
brow, a bill inquiring pure air ahead.
Got all that? Good show. Things are looking up.

III.   Conder
We stick to it through boredom, attrition
of camp life. Requests for proper walkways
over mud, a supply of clean water,
provoke sullen prolonged hut searches. Behind
the huts cesspools of discharged latrines spread.
Elsewhere new names rise: Stalingrad, Tobruk.

IV.   Waterston
The Roman soothsayers studied their cries
and movements for knowledge of the future,
the fragile heart's hidden truths. Old as runes
or hieroglyphs, in their mysteries
our instinctive reach for restoration
still finds hope. Augur. From *avis*. A bird.

You soon forget paper, pencil, posture.
The sky draws you to itself. To yourself.
They come, pass like writing on sand but stir
a gratitude pure and undirected
as a showering of light. And at night
sleep like a bird-wing slips over my eyes.

THE LURE

Caroline Hawkridge

1

With such eyesight,
the hooded hawk sees
the unseen as nothing
that needs
imagining.

We believe.

2

Peregrine sits on man's fist, Dutch-hooded,
eye-calm to the whining propeller.

They ride tall in his sky-saddle, three miles above
the tree-barnacled whalebacks of islands.

Released into the slipstream, she levels just
off the wingtip, watching a pair of men.

She waits for their stoop.

Day after day they fall the hurtling blue
until the cameraman's helmet-lens fathoms

her: feet dawdling the wind
above a man-weight with face-skin

ragging like a flag, as he drops
the leaded lure.

Shoulder at the door of the world,
sky flows through her like ink.

WINGS, PLANES AND WEATHER VANES

Joy Winkler

Huddled in seasonal plumage
we move into the slipstream of slow traffic,
join the migration to lakes and frozen valleys.
I peck fretfully at your foibles,
you preen a little in the rear-view mirror.
The weather vane points North.

Some plane's vapour maps a route
in the other direction to a warmer winter.
It's all a matter of personal choice.
A magpie stiffens its wings,
marks the space between us,
makes like a crucifix or a blessing.

GRANDPARENTS

Ruth Symes

Their daughter thought they'd like it –
Moving south from their Lancashire terrace
Albeit less than twenty miles.

In the event, the bungalow was alien to them.
Wide sunlight gushed through the windows, drowning them.
The open-plan lawns supposed a different sort of life.

In the garden, the greenhouse smelt of tomatoes,
A thrush sang, and things grew mercilessly.
The overflowing water-butt always needed skimming.

Inside, Grandpa cooked and cleaned the taps to perfection
With carbolic soap. At mealtimes he swayed
And whistled as if still on the footplate.

In the end, Nana sat atrophied in her chair,
Her angular body at odds with the world,
Her mind ran hither and thither, mocking her lame leg.

But their daughter thought they'd like it,
So she put up a mirror for them to watch the road.
In it, their granddaughters circled round on bikes.

THE HISTORY DEPARTMENT

Anne-Marie Biggs

(I) The Professor

I see myself sometimes as others do, crabbed
over my books, computer stubbornly turned
off; a relic from another age. I am one of many,
a tiny dot of statistical ink marking out the path
for my generation. Here I am at the end, resisting
retirement for another seductive collaboration.
I am what I was meant to be. So grown, sown and
unseeded, feeding on the ambition of my age.
Survival in another place with the means to face
my days alone. I teach a desiccated history to
hopeful children hung over on first freedoms,
glowing and senseless as this rope of past events
binds them to a narrowing world. Once I threaded
up the jewels of another life, when I dozed in
water meadows and watched the hares dancing. I
brought my necklace here, set it on my shelf: an
emerald collar of photographic print, unchanging,
harsh and remote as the moon. Laughing,
smiling into a blind lens. I looked at myself in
the future and never knew.

(II) The Student

I love this place. You'd think that history
is about dead people, but here we are alive
and kicking. The past is always changing,
shifting faster than I can follow. Facts,
evidence, customs, society – they all stream
out towards me, full of sweat and stink and

hunger and power. I am giddy with this
opening world; I wish I could hold it all inside
and feel its muscles flexing into my flesh. The
strands of lives once lived and rewritten countless
times; there is no fixed point. We sway here with
them and sense ourselves toppling under the
weight of all those voices. I hand in my assignment
to the secretary; she is lumpy and pregnant. I have
to tell her my name twice. Then I go to see my
tutor, my professor; I sit in one of her velvet armchairs,
like coming home. I can see the photograph of her
with a young man, among the rushes and heat of
some long-ago summer. They are laughing, brimful
of light and I think, that is the life I would like.

AN ORPHAN AT THIRTY SIX

Barbara Holliday

Aware of the imminent closing of your life's door,
You instructed which songs, clothes and even who should mourn.
Told me not to forget to tell so and so you'd gone,
Still to send your Christmas cards and gifts to everyone,
To return unworn shoes and clothes to the catalogue,
Clearly asked there to be no church, mosque or synagogue.
'The Crematorium will do fine, it did your Dad.
Although it will surely make your eldest Aunty sad …
Nothing about God, civil ceremony's just fine.
Make sure you lay on a good spread and plenty of wine.'

I did as I was told and I did you rather proud.
How lovely you looked in your purple and lilac shroud.
As Dolly sang 'And I will always love you' I cried.
Later on, Aunty Phyllis rang to tell me that you'd died.
I said 'I know, I was with her.' She asked 'Who is this?'
She was mortified; rang the wrong person on her list.

I cleared out your flat and insisted on solitude.
Allowing anyone to see your smalls would be rude.
Gave all of your furniture to charity collection.
Thought about using your prized sideboard as a coffin.

You taught me that sadness can be conquered by laughter.
It's the best advice you could have given a daughter.
I think of you always, across my face spreads a smile.
And I sit and hug your memory in my mind for a while.

ICON

Peter Branson

For B. L.

The photo re-appears, a centre-piece,
reframed, enshrined, as radiant as the day
immortalised, though more than ten years past.
Petite, her shy smile bracketed by long
blond hair, he mentions her occasionally:
'Soul mates.' Soon after it begins (they click
at work: she's forty-three and married, grown
up kids, he's childless and divorced), she has
a mammogram, routine. He drives her round
to hear the news. Later he waits outside
the ward until her family has been.
He soldiers on, as people do, gets by,
yet knows the man he was, twenty again,
invincible, when she was his, has died.

JAZZ ON NINE ELEVEN

Rob Blaney

Before the storm, birds shower the trees and
fall silent as woodcuts,
though he doesn't notice, being tuned to jazz,
the bleat of horns, the traffic of the rush hour
winding up to a bop crescendo.
And lest his temper snaps he taps his foot
to the rhythm of a passing truck, boards the train.
No time for goodbyes,
just a collision of whispers,
a text message, apologies;
and downbeat, he mimes a favourite riff:
a chorus from Duke's 'Magenta Haze;'
leaves the platform still spinning the melody
until the escalator busks another line,
and rocks him noisily through sliding doors
in mute-sealed rooms,
to his office in steel cortex.

Emails dance.
His shredder gnaws at yesterday's mistakes;
the atrophy of a another tedious day begins:
flab of paper, squeal of fax,
and, distracted by hiss of coffee machine,
he wonders why she's left him,
waits as her face shrinks from screensaver,
clicks at globes in distant worlds,
drums a twelve bar on the keys.
And above the aircon's calm throb

He is oblivious to growl of walking bass,
fat chords, brass screams

as aircraft skim glass ceilings
with sonic booms.

MASSAGE

George Horsman

It jumps to attention like a cinema seat
vacated as I lie on your table, those slim
Adriatic hands kneading their rhythms and tides
along the narrow seaway of my limbs,
my body silhouetted as the Apennines.
The towel's white Alp prods to a single peak.

But all's below the knee, no higher – masseuses
have their guideropes, too – and never lower
than the crumple of waist massif. Your pressing
starts a slow fall of words – mere few, in summer's
wrestle with sweat. We are detached, demure.
The Matterhorn rises unseen, my eyes, like yours,
not noticing.

TEMPLE GARDEN

Jonathan Musgrove

Pink, succinct,
Spiked globes on sticks
Raised above the drum.

Crimson, thick
As syrup.
Dragons dart
In flight

And the unremitting heat
Is softened by a breeze.

Light and shade,
Never more pronounced,
And the golden moss
Dries on the stone.

CROSSING: 1946

Russell Morris

With hints of old-style European
she recreates the grand departures of all apprehensive heroines:
white gloves waving from the stern,
above a weight of water revolving,
milling sea-lace
for a ship of brides.

She re-pins a little of the north Atlantic breeze.

She will not know austerity when she arrives:
she will wear fur,
she will taste fresh coffee
and she will eat her corn sweet and ripe from the cob.

The handrail shudders on deck:
below, dark engines
and worrisome turbulence.
How did she not hear the great machine throughout her years?
Or realise that fine work
such as the tulle of love and marriage
can be rent in an instant?

CROSBY SANDS – AN IRON MAN SPEAKS

Ellis Lloyd

Why cast me in this melodrama
Of bird smoke and torn sky?
Only to watch the waves, the Welsh
And the great bulk ships passing?
The only thing I'll get is barnacles.

I'm dwarfed by the freeport cranes,
Naked to swinging wind-farm sabres.
Now he says he loves windmills;
Turned his coat to anti-Quixote
And me an anti-Sancho Panza.

But that's mega-sculptors for you,
How they fake little David up
Until he swells Goliath size.

This one broadcasts himself like seed.
'Hoc est corpus meum.' Oh really?
Just who does he think he is?

He's never cut out for a God –
Just a rusting diaspora of Everyman
Fecklessly strolling away to sea.

His wife could say, 'I'll flit too,
Strand him while the bandages harden.'
(That'd be terminal for all these
Container trips of his precious essence.)

And it's a thinning essence too.
Read my wrist-tag – sixty-eight
Out of a hundred dilute siblings.

I'm stiff and locked, but look how
The found art flows at my feet,
For instance, this random branch,
Gnarled by the love-licks of the sea,
These sand-curls in carved infinities,
The elegant sweep of the sculpted shore,
The curves beach-combed by the wind.
I can't show a grain of their grace.

I'm only here for Gormleyists
To nod their knowing heads and gawp
And every child to point and giggle.

But let me ask you (in spite of him)
What's the most you can leave behind?
Just the exact shape of an absence.

HELSBY IN WINTER SUN

Ellis Lloyd

Stand here on Helsby Crag
Old desert lion, crouching
Scrub-maned and red-browed,
Paws resting in Mersey mud.

His stone frown is the guard
For fox covert and pine wood
Sheepfold and close orchard
Bean field and cottage plot.

His watch is over no-man's-land
Road-trenched – six lanes of it
Flowing and pulsing with the blood
Of leisure and coloured commerce.

Rails still gleam here. Once
A steam dragon reared from the earth
To roar and lunge across the Weaver.
Now the scuffed diesel crawls.

Chemical spires close at hand
Glint and splinter the sun, drinking
Old ooze from time-pressed swamps.
The lazy sky wheels on a gull.

Cooling towers grind away
To pack the air with solid vapour.
Daresbury tower is prising out
Secrets clenched in the fist of God.

Out there the banked sea-road flows
Drowsing now, almost shipless.

Cathedrals at the far horizon
Pray and strive, pointing at God.

Wide-shouldered, the road thrusts on,
Swaggering to defeated Wales,
Lusting to find Sunday pleasure
And roister among the dumb chapels.

AT JODRELL BANK

David Selzer

The radio telescope trundles on rails
in a landscape of dairy cows and ponds,
tuning into the dispersing cosmos.
The universe is replete with sound. We
fill it with meaning and impedimenta.
Star sailors embark on metaphor
and intricate engines. We record
the energy of suns dead longer than
dinosaurs. We listen to stars yet
tolerate hunger – and we stare still
into the black wonder of starry nights.
Like addicts, we exploit experience.
The ether is redolent with humankind,
our majestic jabber.

WARRINGTON BANK QUAY

Catherine Bruton

Sitting on the platform, forty minutes early –
as usual. 'In case the swing-bridge was up,'
my mum always said (though it never was).
The train is late – again – and children,
'Should always offer seats to taller folks,'
according to my dad, who stands and eyes
the yellow line on the platform like an electric fence,
bristling with potentially hazardous currents.
My sister and I sit on our rucksacks, bottoms squelched
against canvas bulging with pencils and toys and colouring books
('To keep us quiet on the journey') and squish sandwiches warm
and soggy against our holiday clothes and wriggle
on our pin-cushion needle-cushion bums
and daren't complain.
My little brother is stepping over lines,
and my sister is sulking, which seems to be what
you do when you are big. My mum is fretting about connections
at Birmingham, and whether or not she turned the cooker off but
my Dad just keeps staring at the yellow line
as if it is a short fuse
with a small flame creeping along it, closer and closer
to the round black bomb that might go off.
Anytime.
Suddenly.
If it reaches the end of something called a tether.
So, I
stare at the chimneys.
The big silver chimneys
that tower above the station. They look
like a princess palace, made of silvery dragon scales which
gleam in the sun, but I hear
my mum telling my brother (whose anty pants make him squirm and

fidget ever closer to the yellow fuse line) that they make soap
        flakes there,
in the silver chimneyed factory behind platform 3.
I lift my nose and suck hard and I can smell the sweet sour scent of
cooked washing powder, like burnt laundry,
or a bar of soap left out to melt on the tarmac driveway
(we did that with a box of crayons once and all the colours
melded into one rainbow and my mum had to throw them away
        before
my dad saw them and got cross). I
inhale again and
sneeze. And I imagine soap flakes,
like white snowflakes (no two flakes are the same, you know) floating
up from the chimneys and rising skywards
(why does snow always fall down?)
towards the clouds that are their home. Like
a homecoming.

Now, thirty years away, I sit
on a train, also coming home. And, because old habits
die hard, I get up from my seat at Crewe,
even though
it no longer takes the full twenty minutes
to gather up all my stuff (no felt-tip pen lids
hidden beneath neighbouring seats or dolls' stray shoes
shoved behind upholstery – or, once, up my brother's nose). But
I still get up and stand
by the exit, 'So there won't be a last minute rush,' and
I raise a three-fingered salute
to the eight cooling towers at Fiddler's Ferry, still sitting, crouched
on the marshes like giant squatting toads. (Who came up
with the idea of the salute? Was it my sister
who said there were trolls living inside them? Or was it dragons?)
I'm suddenly sad because I can't remember. And then,
I see the gleaming silver of the Lever Brothers' soap factory and
I tug down the window and stick my head out to feel the rushing

Wind on my face and I feel reckless,
even now, hearing still the voice of my dad (in whose memory I
will never put a knife in a toaster or leave candles unattended)
        telling me
that I could get my
head sliced off if we encounter an approaching train, or, heaven
forbid,
a tunnel. I hear his voice reprimand me and I think
of yellow lines
and short fuses
and family holidays he endured rather than enjoyed.
And I understand the quiet pain and patience it must have taken
to remain – mostly – behind those yellow lines.
I inhale the sweet sharp tang of the soap suds and wish
I'd asked him to explain to me how they make soap.
Because he would have known. And perhaps would have enjoyed
        telling me.
As the train nears the station, the smell of burnt soap envelops me,
Hits me.
Like a hug on a station platform.
A homecoming.

QUARRY

Philip Williams

Once, we stopped, left our bikes, stripped
and swam covertly in the red clay-pit
we called the Quarry. Drying on its bank,
we looked back across its piers and poles,
those barbed wire strands,
that dorsal fin of corrugated iron,
compared our cocks and balls.

Of course, we dared not tell our parents
as they'd neither dared tell theirs.
It all lies buried now, sunk without trace
beneath breeze-block and concrete,
dredged of its iron, its drowned boys
circling blind and deep beneath our feet
to clutch us had we swum there longer.

DUKE'S CLOUGH

Angela Topping

Leaving the copse, walking back to bikes,
feet snag on ruts. Glancing back

from here, it's nothing much,
just trees, battered by the motorway.

'Come on,' says dad, 'it's time to go.'
Back to the fusty house for Sunday tea.

Brambles snatch our slacks, fruitless hooks
fragmenting the track as we climb.

Armfuls of bluebells powder the air,
cool and woody, intoxicating as whispered words.

Thrushes threaten their neighbours in syllabics.
Crass cars tune up through engines' scales.

As the bike's pedals respond to weight and time
the clough is lost to us, a closed fist, a shut eye.

FOG

Peter Howard

The girls had been dancin'
so they had, so they had.

Jigs and reels and the like
in some competition in Crewe
or somewhere
where trains laboured
late into a night
when a '60s fog stopped them in their tracks,
so to speak.

The same fog that spread its hand
across my father's face as he paced
from kitchen to road
from road to kitchen
fear spreading like diphtheria
as the whisky prayers
and 'please-God' promises
were chanted,
whispered,
then answered
as they appeared

grey ghosts at our door
swept inside.

SALT

Andrew Bailey

The capers come saltpacked and instantly the crystals
spirit me seasons back to Tudor-timbered streets
of my single figures, to Romans and their salaries

in the museum and me making them armour from chickenwire,
papier-maché and primary-school vim. Bosses from salt dough
and Hammerite. Crammed in the jar as preservative

it becomes a million madeleines, as if it has kept
this memory fresh for resurfacing now, it clears the frost
from my path, brings its glassy setts into microscope focus.

I have married a woman who favours salt over sugar,
who has brought me far south and salted my tail to be tame
to this new house, new life, near the seawater

that crisps in sunlight on my hands like dried poster paint
from a newspaper breastplate. Still some salt of my youth,
incorruptible, in me rising to recognise its caper-packed twin.

There is joy in me I had forgotten, it swells through me like brine
through pork belly, and were I alone by the fridge
I would kiss this small jar. It is salt, after all, that cures.

A FOURTH DIMENSION

Alison Leonard

Salt flats between tide and cloud
and the only movement, of water:
salt up, fresh down. It seeps between
wide banks, cuts through pressed earth.
A pale foal nuzzles under its russet mother.
Sand shifts under a lizard.
A lapwing floats. Gorse stirs.

A cry. It is a wizard's wand, parting
the marram grass, and sheep flow through.
Among them, a girl carries a pup:
four wide eyes. Whistle – sharp,
instructive – and the tide is fully sprung.
Moons could not pull it steadier,
more urgent through the dunes,

this sheep river flowing parallel
to the tide, contrary, across land. In this
maze of creeks, each footfall is a new
discovery for the single mind of sheep.

How are they led? By gravity? It is
the dog and her man. At the tip
of the invisible wand, far by
twenty creeks and an arc of sky,
the dog becomes the man's thrown half.
Full mother to her future in the girl's
arms, she is the season's engine for
this flow, this need to pass time on.

A tear in the woollen fabric.
Two sheep have strayed.

The dog chases –
terror scatters foal from mare,
lapwing parents from their young.
A farther cry – a second whistle –
the wizard has reined her, and the dog
lies low… swerves gently round … This
thrown magic re-knits the plait
and the sheep flow whole.

The pup is running now beside the girl.
Lapwing lands. Foal feeds. Gorse stirs.

SHEEP

Sheila Powell

Sheep nibble on nothing,
Graze the air,
Grow fat on frozen fields
And the five o'clock shadow
Of razored fells.
Sheep expect nothing –
Tolerate everything
Winter and weather can bring.
How then are their lambs so full of spring?

RECALL

Angi Holden

Later, I remembered headlights sweeping
across the rutted moorland
and the blue, intermittent glow that traced
the roadway snaking through the heather.

The waiting; yes, I was aware of that.
And the sudden shock of unfamiliar sounds:
the rush of grinding steel, the hiss of steam
and softer, almost swallowed by the fog,
a lingering moan.

A metallic taste, too. An expectation
of a filling shaken loose, or else
a fragment of enamel, a fractured
cusp exposing old amalgam.

But most of all, the eyes. I recall
the medic, his backward glance, brief and weary
as they lifted you, oh, so gently; the trucker, the one
who stopped to help and then broke down and wept.

And beyond the hawthorn hedge, three sheep
swaying as they chewed, their yellow gazes
wary, watchful, timeless.

HOREB

Robbie Burton

Fence-posts lead into
        and out of Lake Horeb
barbed wire linking
        one buzzard-perch to another.
No burning bushes
        no springs struck from rock
but mountain ash lit by
        a thousand fiery drops
and limestone awash
        with sunlight and mica.
Dog-splash and ripple-tune
        rise from the shallows
slaloming thermals
        alongside the swallow.
Somewhere in title-deeds
        fence-posts divide water.

DODO

Jonny Reid

The Dodo exists in my house
beneath revision and lad mags.
It is in 'near-good' condition
once you've rolled it all out
like you're Long John Silver.
The Dodo stands on the dining table.

I drew it when I was eight
and to see it again,
revived and life-size in crayon
standing on sugar paper,
reminds me that once
I was dressed in maroon

in a room full of maroon
dwarves jostling for the best pens,
bickering over pictures of lions
and elephants, one of them screeching
for the toilet like a parrot,
his face turning tropical.

My hands open a textbook
that claps upon the table
with its weight,
then I hoist each page
and they flap flap flap
until I glimpse it under D:

The Dodo. Flightless
bird of Mauritius,
extinct by 1681,
through animals brought

to its island by man;
pigs smiling with yellow lips.

I roll up my sleeves,
maroon riddled with holes
courtesy of my milk teeth
that feel like a joke,
one of the molars
I can shift with a lick.

Hovering over my seat
I recreate the ancient bird
with an ammo belt of crayons.
It's time consuming
as I arrange the paper
with my struggling range.

And I wave my colours
over the white, bringing him back,
beak and sorry tail: feeble wings
tucked into grey feathers
as he waltzes his way
through ferns that shiver.

The island is designed
around him: a paradise
of sun, sea and sand
and the tide is drawn

from beyond the edge.
His bill is closed.

The bell rang
and I sprinted home
and chased him up the stairs
where he flew zigzag

to soar on my gallery wall
(with assistance).

Dodo. Small
and magnificent.
I remember
as I roll everything up
and slide you back
into the glossy jungle.

MENDING YOUR GUITAR

John Davies

Curve of its side stoved
as if a drum skin torn,
splintered to the size of a fist
that could never again fit
in the cradle of your arm.
Its wood, long given up
your tobacco scent,
specks of your skin now mingle
in the frets with mine.
Touch almost too light,
almost too heavy –
all you could do
but to hold onto its neck
as your chords crashed, roared
and dragged you away, upwards.
The final string you snapped
on that last whiskey and raging night
still resounding.
No more late nights, no loud guitar.
You promised.
Patched up now,
your broken machine
resurrected into new songs
I can hear you singing.

YEATS EXHIBITION

John Davies

The voices of actors on endless repeat
as if every word somewhere
always being spoken,
always being heard –
we moved between his manuscripts
projected onto screens reeling
Sligo scenes and ancestors raised
like cheap-trick spectres
by magicians in music halls.
Made sure they were scribbled over,
any words meant to blindside
or to deceive – shot through
and left in his wake.
The bare museum pieces
sealed not to shatter to dust.
This his last pair of glasses,
lock of his hair.
Held in the crypt
of this crisp Dublin day.
This the page his hand moved across.
This his unused love.

MY GRANDDAD BURIES KING AT SOUTER LIGHTHOUSE

Jake Campbell

I can see him pulling
up at Souter. Beam
of the lighthouse scanning
the bonnet of his Escort estate
as he opened the boot, lifted out
the rug-rolled corpse, delicate
as a pile of firewood.

Wellying the spade
into the grass, I imagine that others
passing along Coast Road,
after nightshifts and engagements
in car parks – too tired or tireless
to care – will have seen him:
mosquito to England's neckline.

The radio might have been on,
the passenger door ajar as 'Golden Brown'
sprinkled out of the stereo.
Three feet down, he'll have wiped
his brow with a shirt sleeve,
dug the spade in like a flag-pole,
lifted the corpse of King
into a pore of the earth.

Refilling the hole would have been
the easy part, the headstone
the problem. Rolling the rock
over the mud blemish, he must have
cursed the stupid mutt for dying.

Back in his car, slipping the gearbox
into third as he growled up Lizard Lane,
the sun opening over the North Sea
like a tangerine, he'll have begun singing:
'Golden brown, texture like sun,
lays me down with my mind; he runs …'.

LUNET (FRICTION DRUM)

Judy Ugonna

Now that you are silent,
how will the dead ones dance to freedom?

The wooden wedges
of your three-tongued drum
whispered a blend of notes
that echoed wood-wind tones
of forest, rain and cloud
as the drummers tapped and stroked,
coaxing your rippling sound
over the burial ground.

You summoned the dead ones
from their graves, drumming them
free from their bones
to the lands of the spirits.
You told the living to let go
the years of mourning
as they raised the dust
with dancing feet.

Now that you are silent,
how will the dead ones dance to freedom,
how will the living let them go?

SLIT DRUM

Judy Ugonna

A knot of people
came to my hut,
spent the day
in tricks,
checking my second sight,
testing the truth of my drum.

Mute at last
they tendered
a little necklace –
stained silver beads
and a single piece
of butter-coloured amber.

I held it up,
eyed it, inhaled it,
kept it by me while I slept.
They sat in wait.
The necklace muttered
ceaselessly in my ear.

At day's break, sick,
I spat the tale
into the belly of
my drum,
tapped out the truth
in their faces.

The slit drum made
its announcement.
They slipped away in shame,
to see to it.

JAKE

Jonny Reid

The Jack Russell terrier
with a yellow pencil trapped in his jaw
runs between our arguments – we stop
our mouths, caught by the sight of him
as he paws, bows and scribbles on the lino

To you both

I just can't do this anymore.

Regards,

Jake.

He exits the cat flap

flap-flap flap.

TEENAGERS IN LOVE

Vikki Littlemore

I chant superstitious rhymes
and stretch chest muscles for you,
watch teenagers in the sun,
tangled arms and tongues
at bus stops.
I walk past, thirty-two.

I watch as other girls with bigger breasts
suck the wet lips of disposable men;
the same white light in the sky,
shining like something other than the moon.

In the fragmented, opium flame and glare of sun,
in the silk-soft gilded green and bird song
of warm and cool afternoon;
gently softened skin exudes the absorbed
heat of the day. Skin: soft, lush as the watered grass,
tender under the palm of *him*, whose palms are
somewhere else, wandering over someone else's
skin with borrowed caresses,
cupping undeserving shoulders,
drinking the evening in ignorance
on benches or in the burning flare
of back-gardens; next to hosepipes,
trees. Tiny red spiders on thighs.
And *we*, in garden chairs with pens
blooming and fizzing
with impotence and futility,
cup the shoulders no-one will.
And wait.

SNAGGING

Michael Scully

He would light another Woodbine to help
resolve a problem with the job in hand.
Thumbed chin, screwed eyes, two fingered.
Cogitating out loud and teaching me, the child.

I would wish for too wet for working rain
to drive us into the closeness of the shed
with all the smells of swan wood, oiled tools
and him, his coal tar soap and cigarettes.

I would gaze in awe at the cannon ball
biceps beneath the stretched white skin
and long to stoke the sawdust from the
brambled arms. Such strong arms!

Strong arms that never hit me once or,
maybe even worse, never held me close.

GERRIS LACUSTRIS (COMMON POND SKATER)

Helen Clare

It turns out that the knack my mother had
(in best dress and bare feet) of bouncing smoothed stones
off the surface of Lake Bala, depends
on water meshing, like a trampoline
returning the fallen to the sky
or the atmosphere pushing off spacecraft.

So, water clings to itself like mercury,
avoiding air, forming drops as it's sloughed
from drenched dogs. Insect legs stretch the water's shell,
they paddle without piercing or wetness.

It's true too that a mosquito's footfall
does not break dreams, as the skin, oblivious
to air, shrugs off the countless touches
of the day. Talk to me now about ripples.

ANAX IMPERATOR (EMPEROR DRAGONFLY)

Helen Clare

Have you seen the monster on the windowsill?
There it is, in 100 mil. measuring jug
sealed with Clingfilm: oaky brown and brittle,
a battering ram face and stumpy wings,
its empty abdomen an armoured hose
of overlapping scales. The integument
of a nymph. I came here after my divorce.

My parents tended me with food, bundled me
in to the back seat and drove me to still places,
waited and for the nth time watched me leave.
Now I sit with them on the old settle,
as they shed the stories of all their selves
into the pale light from beyond the pond,
and see the encroaching stiffness in their hands.